You N... Monkey!

Written by Michael Coleman

Illustrated by Tim Warnes

Monkey was a noisy monkey.

"Chitter-chatter,
chitter-chatter,
eeh-ah-ooh!"

Lion was peacefully sleeping
until he heard...

"Chitter-chatter,
chitter-chatter,
eeh-ah-ooh!"

"Be quiet, you noisy monkey!"
roared Lion.
"I'm trying to sleep."

Elephant was quietly talking
until she heard...

"Chitter-chatter,
chitter-chatter,
eeh-ah-ooh!"

"Be quiet, you noisy monkey!"
bellowed Elephant.
"I'm trying to talk."

Hippo was silently thinking
until he heard...

"Chitter-chatter,
chitter-chatter,
eeh-ah-ooh!"

"Be quiet, you noisy monkey!"
honked Hippo.
"I'm trying to think."

Monkey was sad.
"I'll go where no one
can hear me
'Chitter-chatter,
chitter-chatter,
eeh-ah-ooh!'"

Monkey climbed
to the top
of the highest tree
in the jungle.
And there he saw
a raging fire!
"It's coming this way,"
Monkey said,
as he raced
down the tree
to warn his friends.

Lion was still peacefully sleeping until he heard...

"Chitter-chatter.

Chitter-chatter.

FIRE! FIRE!

FIRE!"

Now Lion was really angry.

"I'll get you, you noisy monkey!"
roared Lion,
as he chased Monkey
through the jungle.

Elephant was still quietly talking until she heard...

"Chitter-chatter.

Chitter-chatter.

FIRE! FIRE!

FIRE!"

Now Elephant was really angry.

"I'll get you, you noisy monkey!"
bellowed Elephant,
as she chased Monkey
through the jungle.

Hippo was still silently thinking until he heard...

"Chitter-chatter.

Chitter-chatter.

FIRE! FIRE!

FIRE!"

Now Hippo was really angry.

"I'll get you, you noisy monkey!"
honked Hippo,
as he chased Monkey
through the jungle.

Monkey ran faster and faster with Lion, Elephant and Hippo right behind him.

"We'll get you, you noisy monkey!" they all cried.

Monkey ran until
he reached the river.
Then he pointed at the fire
they had all escaped from.

"Chitter-chatter.

Chitter-chatter.

FIRE! FIRE!

FIRE!"

Lion looked.
Elephant looked.
Hippo looked.
They all saw that
Monkey had saved them.

Well done,
you noisy
monkey!